PUUUNG

편 안 하 고
사랑스럽고
그   래

Love is··· 2

편안하고 사랑스럽고 그래 2

초판 1쇄 발행 2016년 8월 16일
개정판 1쇄 발행 2020년 4월 2일
개정판 6쇄 발행 2024년 12월 15일

지은이 퍼엉
펴낸이 최순영
출판1 본부장 한수미
라이프 팀장 곽지희

펴낸곳 ㈜위즈덤하우스 **출판등록** 2000년 5월 23일 제13-1071호
주소 서울특별시 마포구 양화로 19 합정오피스빌딩 17층
전화 02) 2179-5600 **홈페이지** www.wisdomhouse.co.kr

ⓒ 퍼엉, 2020

ISBN 979-11-90630-81-8 04810
      979-11-90630-82-5 (세트)

편안하고
사랑스럽고
그   래

Love is··· 2

글·그림 퍼엉

위즈덤하우스

일러스트레이터
퍼엉입니다

'편안하고 사랑스럽고 그래' 2권 출간 이후 오랜 시간이 지났습니다. 그동안 제겐 많은 변화가 있었어요. 학교를 졸업하고, 새로운 장소로 이사를 하고, 감당하기 어려운 여러 이별을 경험하고, 새로운 언어를 배우고, 여러 취미도 만들었어요. 물론 전혀 변하지 않은 것들도 있어요. 그중 하나가 그림이지요.

여전히 제 일상은 그림 그리는 일로 가득 차 있어요. 매일 배경 자료를 보고, 일러스트를 그리고, 애니메이션을 만들고 있어요. 변하지 않은 것들 중 가장 감사한 부분이기도 하지요. '편안하고 사랑스럽고 그래' 시리즈를 5년이나 그렸지만 아직도 그리고 싶은 것들이 많아요. 그래서 요즘 '내가 나를 잘 몰랐다'는 생각이 들어요.

저는 어렸을 적부터 말주변이 참 없었어요. 남들과 이야기를 나누는 게, 정확히는 제 이야기를 남에게 하는 것이 부담스러웠어요. 상황이 이렇다 보니, 저는 제가 말하는 걸 별로 좋아하지 않는 사람이라고 생각했어요. 누군가에게 내 그림을 보여주는 일이, 내 이야기를 들려주는 일이라는 것을 몰랐던 것이죠. 이것을 깨닫고 나니 제 속에 들어앉은 엄청난 수다쟁이가 보여요. 그리고 또 그려서 사람들에게 여러 이야기를 들려주고 싶어 하는 이야기꾼이 여기 있습니다. 앞으로 제 속의 수다쟁이가 어떤 이야기를 풀어낼지 계속 지켜봐주시면 좋겠습니다.

I am Puuung,

an illustrator

It has been a long time since the second volume of 'Love is...' series was published. There were many changes to me in the meanwhile. I graduated from university. I moved to a new house. I had to experience several goodbyes beyond my control. I learned a new language. I had new hobbies too. Of course, some don't change at all. One of them is painting.

My daily life is still filled with painting. I search for background resources, paint illustrations, and produce an animation day after day. I'm most grateful for that among what hasn't changed. I have painted illustrations of this series for 5 years, but there are still plenty more. Now I see that I didn't know myself.

I'm awkward in speaking from childhood up. I feel uncomfortable talking with other people, especially telling my story to them. I couldn't help considering myself as a person of few words. I didn't know that showing my illustrations is telling my stories. Now that I realized it, I see a very talkative person in me. The person, who want to tell many stories through many illustrations, is here. I hope that you will continue to look forward to stories which the chatterer in me would depict from now on.

최 고 의
피 로 회 복 제

"피곤해 보여요.

　맛있는 거 먹고 기운 냈으면 좋겠어요!"

"네가 만들어주는 음식이

　최고의 피로 회복제예요!!"

Greatest cure for fatigue

"You look tired,

I want you to eat something good and feel better!"

"The food you make is the greatest cure for

fatigue!!"

팔 베 개

깨우러 왔다가 팔 베고 자요.

Arm pillow

I came to wake you but ended up falling asleep on your arm.

얼른 물놀이 하러 가요!

"일어나요! 얼른 물놀이 하러 가요!"
"벌써? 아직 오전인데…"

Let's hurry to the water!

"Wake up! Let's go play in the water!" "Already? It's still too early…"

예 쁘 게 그 려 줄 게 요

이렇게 뽀뽀해주는 거 그려 주세요.

I'll draw a nice portrait of you

Draw us kissing like this.

노 래 를
불 러 요

"난나나나나 나난나나 난나나나나 나나봐♬"
음치도 가수가 되는 이 순간!
나 홀로 목욕하는 시간은 즐거워요!

Singing

"Lalalalalalalalalalalalalalalala"

The moment when a terrible singer sounds beautiful!

I enjoy my time in the bath!

저 녁
7 시

알록달록한 하늘을 보면서
오늘 하루 있었던 일을 이야기해줘요.

7 PM

Looking at the colorful sky We talk about our day.

왜 여기서 책 보고 있어요?

왜 여기서 책 보고 있어요?
날씨도 좋은데 같이 외출해요!

Why are you reading here?

Why are you reading here? The weather's nice, let's go out!

대
단
하
죠
?

"이거 봐요!"

사과 껍질을 한 번도 안 끊고 깎았어요!

Isn't this amazing?

"Look at this! I peeled the whole apple in one strand!"

춤 출 래 요 ?

"일어나서 같이 춤추시겠어요?"
"좋아요!"

Will you dance with me?

"Will you stand up and dance with me?" "Of course!"

영 상 통 화

영상으로 뽀뽀 쪽!

빨리 보고 싶어요!

Video call

I blow a kiss to you! I can't wait to see you!

생
일

생일 축하해요!

Birthday

Happy birthday!

야
식

야식으로 라면을 끓여 먹었어요.

"내일 얼굴 엄청 붓겠다!"

"그래도 좋아~"

Late-night snack

We eat ramen as a late-night snack. "My face will be so swollen tomorrow!" "It's okay."

소
나
기

장 보고 돌아가는 길에 갑자기 비가 쏟아졌어요.

"빨리 달려요!"

Rain showers

It started pouring on our way back home from grocery shopping.

"Run fast!"

수
박

더운 날엔 수박이 최고예요!

Watermelon

Watermelon is the best on a hot day!

grafolio.com/puuung1

뽕！

창문 밖 풀숲 사이에서 네가 뽕! 나타났어요!

"안녕!"

Boo!

You appeared from the bushes outside the window. "Hi!"

두
리
안

과일의 왕이라고 불리는 두리안을 먹어봤어요.

"웩! 냄새도 이상하고 맛도 끔찍해요!"

"정말? 난 진짜 맛있는데?"

Durian

We ate what is called the king of fruits.

"Ew! It smells and tastes awful!" "Really? I think it's good!"

이
불

이불을 뒤집어쓰고 장난을 쳐요.

Under the covers

We play under the covers.

이 불
굼 벵 이

"우리 아가 일어나요. 저녁 먹어요!"
"나는 아가가 아니에요. 꿈틀꿈틀 이불 굼벵이예요~"

Bed worm

"Get up, baby. Let's eat dinner!" "I'm not a baby. I'm a bed worm."

빵 야

꽃에 물을 주다가 장난을 쳤어요.

"빵야 빵야!"

Pew!

We started joking around while watering the flowers. "Pew! Pew!"

자 는 모 습 을
지 켜 봐 요

그새 또 잠들었어요.

자는 모습도 얼마나 예쁜지 몰라요.

Watching her sleep

She was quick to fall asleep, You don't know how adorable she is when she sleeps.

잇은 거 없어요?

하늘을 보다가 뽀뽀를 했어요.
너무 좋아요!
"그런데 뭐 잊은 거 없어요? 물 끓는 것 같은데!"

Didn't you forget something?

We kiss as we watch the sky.

It's so nice!

"But didn't' you forget something? I think the water is boiling!"

무
서
운

이
야
기

늦은 밤.

불 꺼놓고 무서운 이야기를 해줬어요.

"뒤에서 귀신이 뿅 나타났어!"

"푸하하. 뭐야? 하나도 안 무섭잖아요!"

무서운 이야기에는 소질이 없나 봐요!

Scary stories

Late at night, I told her scary stories in the dark.

"A ghost popped out behind you!"

"Haha. What? That's not scary at all!"

I guess telling scary stories isn't my forte!

작은 영화관

의자에 기대어
함께 영화를 봤어요.

Mini theater

Leaning on the sofa
We watched a movie together.

다 녀 왔 습 니 다

"어서 와요! 보고 싶었어요. 오늘은 어땠어요?"

I'm home

"Welcome back! I missed you. How was your day?"

짠！

짠~

Cheers!

Cheers!

조 금
특 별 한 밤

오늘 밤은 조금 특별했어요. 밖에서 불꽃 축제를 했거든요!
우리는 평소처럼 방 안에서 간식을 먹으며 대화를 했어요.
대화가 잠깐씩 끊길 때마다 밤하늘을 봤어요.
정말 예쁘네요!

A little special night

Tonight was a little special. There were fireworks outside!

We ate snacks and chatted inside like usual.

We peeked at the sky every time we stopped talking.

It was so pretty!

꿈

낯잠을 잤어요.

Dream

We took a nap.

아 이 스 크 림

추운 날 따뜻한 방에서

이불 덮고 아이스크림 먹는 게 최고예요!

Ice cream

On a cold day,

eating ice cream in a warm room Underneath the blanket is the best!

가
을
산
책

산책을 하다가 갑자기 저를 번쩍 안아 올렸어요.

공주님이 된 기분이에요!

Autumn walk

He suddenly picked me up while we walked around. I felt like a princess!

아 이 스 크 림
먹 고 싶 어 요

뿅!

"우리 아이스크림 먹으러 갈까요?"

"좋아요!"

I want to eat ice cream

Pop! "Shall we go to eat ice cream?" "Yeah!"

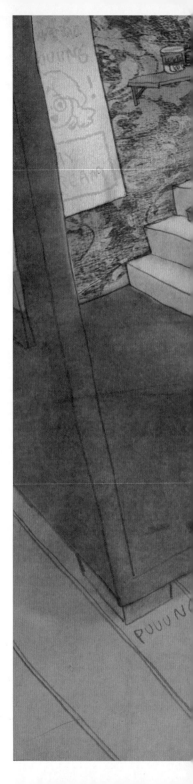

종
이
접
기

동심으로 돌아가 종이접기를 했어요.

Origami

Reminiscing about our childhood, we did origami.

너 의 잠 자 는 모 습

집에 돌아오니 모두 낮잠을 자고 있네요!

자는 모습이 귀여워서 몰래 사진을 찍었어요.

The way you look when you sleep

I came home and everyone was talking a nap!

The way you slept was so cute that I had to take a picture.

아 쿠 아 리 움

아쿠아리움에 놀러 왔어요.
예쁜 해파리를 구경해요!

Aquarium

We came to the aquarium. We observe the pretty jellyfish!

세 수 를 해 요

얼굴을 깨끗이 씻겨주세요~

Face wash

Wash my face squeaky clean, please.

책
을
읽
어
요

"어떤 책이에요?"

"같이 볼래요? 읽어줄까요?"

Reading a book

"What book is that?"

"Do you want to read it together? Do you want me to read it to you?"

놀래 주기

"까꿍!!"

"꺅!!!"

Scaring you

"Peek-a-boo!!" "Ahh!!!"

어 지 러 운
안 경

너의 안경을 써봤어요.
"어지러워요. 눈을 못 뜨겠어!"

Thick glasses

I wore his glasses. "I'm so dizzy, I can't open my eyes!"

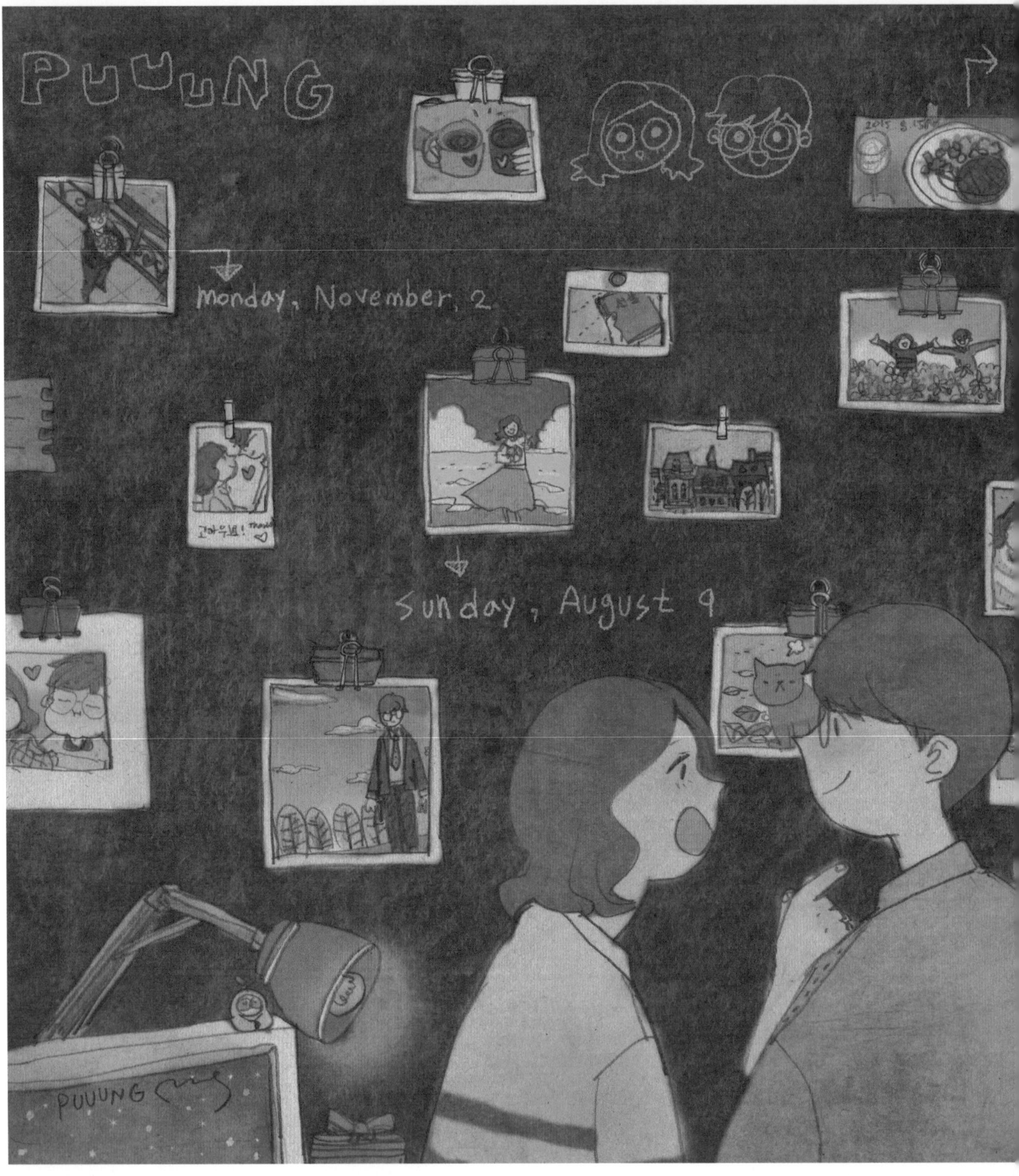
PUUUNG
monday, November, 2
Sunday, August 9
PUUUNG

작 은 전 시 회

그동안 찍었던 사진들을 벽에 붙여
둘만의 전시회를 열었어요.
옛 추억이 새록새록 생각나요.
"이 사진 좀 봐, 이때 정말 웃겼어! 기억나?"

Small exhibition

We had a small exhibition
With the pictures we had taken so far.
We reminisced about our memories.
"Look at this picture, that was so funny! Remember?"

첫 눈
오 는 날 에

"첫눈 오는 날 뭐하고 싶어요?"

"그냥 같이 이불 속에 누워서 푹 자고 싶어요."

On the first day it snows

"What do you want to do on the first day it snows?"

"I just want to sleep well cuddling you in bed."

재
미
있
는

이
야
기

알고 있는 이야기도 네가 말해주면 정말 재미있어요.

Funny story

Stories I already know are still funny when you tell them to me.

다 녀 오 세 요

잘 다녀와요. 쪽!

See you later

See you later. Muah!

밥 먹 는
속 도

"밥 먹는 속도가 느려요!"

"내가 느린 게 아니라 네가 빠른 거야."

우걱우걱~

Speed of eating

"You eat so slowly!" "I'm not slow, you're just fast." Chomp, chomp!

집 으 로 돌 아 가 는 길

눈이 많이 쌓였어요!

On the way home

The snow lay thick!

가필드!
그건 안 돼!

"가필드 그것만은 안 돼!
열심히 준비한 깜짝 선물이란 말이야!"

Garfield! Not that!

"Garfield, anything but that! That's the surprise present I finally made!"

목 도 리 를 만 들 어 요

"완성되면 정말 예쁠 것 같아!
맨날 이 목도리만 하고 다닐 거야."

Knitting a scarf

"It'll be so pretty when it's done! I'm going to wear this scarf every day."

눈
이
와
요

따뜻한 방 안에서 눈이 내리는 하늘을 봐요.

"눈이 많이 많이 쌓였으면 좋겠다."

"그럼 또 눈싸움 하는 거야!"

It's snowing

In a warm room, we watch the sky as the snow falls.

"I hope the snow keeps piling up."

"Then that calls for another snow fight!"

오 늘 저 녁 뭐 예 요 ?

뭐일 것 같아요? 맞춰보세요.

What's for dinner tonight?

What do you think? Try guessing.

저 녁 이 오 기 전

저녁이 오기 직전. 손잡고 어느 옥상을 걸었어요.

"난 이 시간이 좋아요. 하늘 색을 보면 왠지 마음이 울렁울렁 하거든요."

"나도 그래요."

Before it gets dark

We held hands and walked on a rooftop before it got dark.

"I like this moment. The color of the sky somehow makes my heart go pit-a-pat."

"Mine too."

눈 이
와 요

눈밭에 누웠어요.
너랑 함께 있으니
춥게 느껴지지 않고 포근해요.

It's snowing

We lie in a bed of snow.
Being with you
I don't feel cold at all.

연
말
밤

올해의 마지막 밤이에요.

어디 나가지 않고 그냥 테라스에서 과자를 먹었어요.

밤에 먹는 과자는 더 맛있어요!

New Year's Eve

It's the last night of the year. We stay in and eat snacks on the terrace.

Eating snacks at night is so much tastier.

미소가
절로 나요

네가 가까이 오면 히죽히죽 웃음이 나와요.
마냥 좋아요.

Can't help but smile

When you get close, I can't help but smile. I love it.

싸웠어요

싸웠어요.

"흥…."

…사과할까?

We fought

We had a fight. "Hmph…"

… Should I apologize?

겨 울 캠 핑 카

캠핑카 안에서 보드게임을 해요.

"저 숫자는 8 맞지?"

"이 게임 왜 이렇게 잘하는 거예요? 나 몰래 연습했어요?"

Winter car camping

We play board games in a camping car.

"That number is 8, right?" "How are you so good at this game? Did you practice secretly?"

PUUUNG

grafolio.com
/puuung1

PUUUNG

grafolio.com/puuung1

주 물 주 물

어깨 주물러줄게요.

Massaging

I'll massage your shoulders.

무 릎 을
베 고 자 요

무릎을 베고 잠들어요.

"자장가 불러줄까요?"

"뭐? 내가 아기인 줄 알아?

···불러주세요."

Sleeping on your lap

I try to fall asleep on your lap.

"Do you want me to sing you a lullaby?"

"What? Do you think I'm a baby?

…yes."

grafolio.com / puuung1

puuung

소 파 위

소파 위에 앉아 서로를 바라봐요.

그냥요.

조용히 한참을 바라봐요.

On the sofa

We sit on the sofa and look at each other.

Just because. We quietly stare for a while.

꽃 다 발

"선물이에요."
"와, 고마워요. 여기에 예쁘게 심어놓을게!"

A flower bouquet

"It's a gift." "Wow, thank you. I will nicely plant them here!"

호 수 의 밤

눈이 오지 않는 밤, 호수에 나왔어요.

맑게 갠 하늘에서 별이 쏟아지는 것 같아요.

"이 예쁜 장소에 너와 함께 앉아 있는 게 참 좋아!"

Night at the lake

We came out to the lake on a snow -free night. Stars seem to fall from the crystal clear sky.

"I'm so happy to be with you in this beautiful place."

간 식 먹 기 전

달걀이 삶아지길 기다리며 이야기를 해요.

"어어어엄~청 커다란 벌레였다니까! 진짜 무서웠어!"

Before snacking

We tell stories while waiting for the eggs to boil.

"It was a huuuuge bug! It was so frightening!"

좀 이따 봐요

좀 이따 봐요. 쪽!

I'll see you later

See you later. Muah!

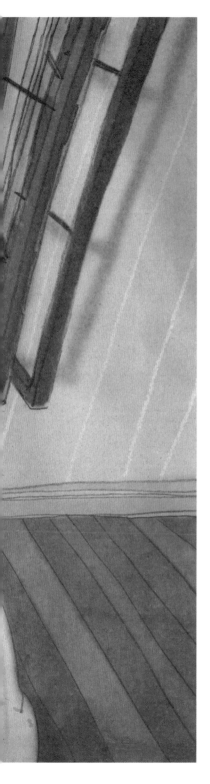

설 레 는
택 배 박 스

"택배 왔어요~ 그저께 주문한 인형이에요."

"정말? 같이 뜯어보자!"

Excited to open the package

"We got a package. It's the doll I ordered the other day."

"Really? Let's open it together!"

음 료
배 달

"음료 배달 왔어요~"

"어서 와요! 무슨 맛으로 사 왔어?"

"당연히 네가 좋아하는 초코 맛이지."

Drink delivery

"I've come to deliver a drink."

"Welcome! What flavor is it?"

"It's your favorite of course, chocolate."

즐거운 대화

해 질 녘, 테라스에 나와서
즐겁게 대화를 나눠요.

A fun talk

At sunset, we come out to the terrace and
Share fun stories.

겨 울 밤

눈이 가득 쌓였어요.

"이대로 밤새 누워 있으면 눈사람이 되겠지?"

"하하. 바보 같은 소리 말고, 이제 들어가요! 우리 따뜻한 코코아 마셔요."

A winter night

Snow is stacked high.

"If we lie here all night, will we become snowmen?"

"Haha, don't be silly. C'mon, let's go inside! Let's have hot chocolate."

PUUNG♥♥ grafolio.com/puuung1

재 미 있 는 거 보 여 줄 게

"푸핫, 이게 저번에 말했던 그거구나!
완전 짱인데?!"

I'll show you something funny

"Oh my, so this is what you talked about last time! Impressive!"

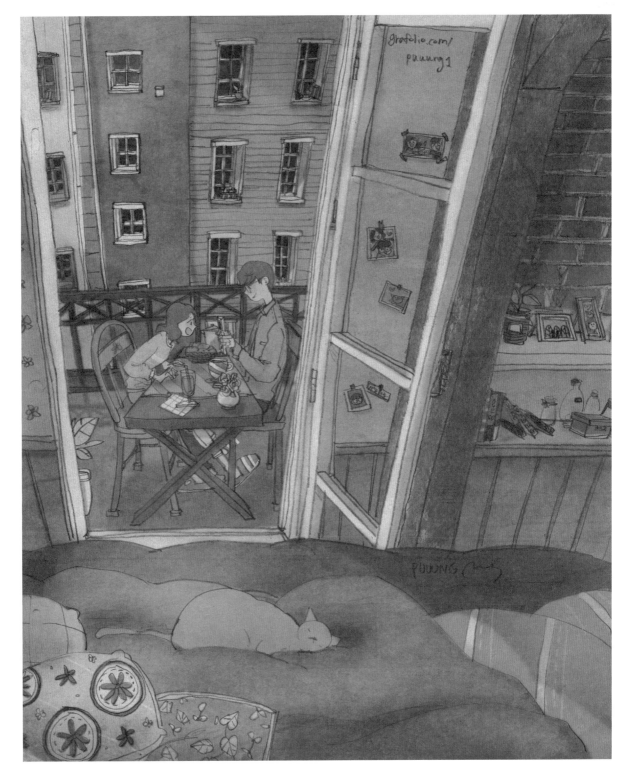

네 가 오 지 않 는 저 녁

올 시간이 훨씬 지났는데 너는 오지 않아요.

"무슨 일이야…"

A night you don't return

It's way past the time you usually come back. "What's going on…?"

바 쁜 날

바쁜 날, 마주보고 앉아 각자 일을 해요.
"가필드, 여기 앉으면 일을 못 한단 말이야~"

Busy day

On a busy day, we sit across from each other and each work alone.

"Garfield, I can't do anything if you sit here."

어떤 옷을 입을까요?

레이스 달린 검은색 원피스는 어때?
너한테 정말 잘 어울릴 것 같아!

What should I wear?

What do you think about this black lace dress?
I think it'd look amazing on you!

Where's he?

Where's he?

나 른 한 아 침

나른한 아침이에요.

"커피 따라 줄게요. 이거 먹고 잠 깨요."

A drowsy morning

It's a drowsy morning. "I'll pour you coffee. Drink this and wake up."

빨 리 올 라 와 요

"나 왔어요! 금방 올라갈게!"

너를 위해 아침부터 준비한 맛있는 음식!

기뻐서 펄쩍펄쩍 뛸 너의 모습을 생각하면 자꾸만 웃음이 나와요.

"빨리 올라왔으면 좋겠다."

Hurry up

"I'm here! I'll be up soon!"

A tasty meal I've been preparing for you since the morning! I laugh at the thought of you jumping in excitement.

"I hope she hurries faster."

나 화났다고!

"나빴어! 아껴 먹으려고 남겨둔 마지막 쿠키를 다 먹어버리다니!

가만 안 둘 거야!"

우걱우걱~

"화내는 모습도 어쩜 이렇게 예쁠까!

이리 와요, 안아줄게. 누가 화나게 했어요?"

I'm mad!

"You're bad! You ate the last cookie I saved! I'm not going to let this slide!"

Crunch, crunch.

"You are so cute even when you are mad! Come here, let me hug you. Who made you angry?"

PUUUNG [ㅎㅎ]

ovafolio.com /puuung1

낮 잠 자 는 너 의 모 습

잠든 너의 모습을 빤히 바라봐요.

The way you look while napping

I gaze at you while you nap.

점심시간 전

엎드려서 책을 읽어요.

"배고프다. 이따가 점심은 뭐 먹을까?"

Before lunch

We lie on our stomachs and read books. "I'm hungry. What should we eat for lunch?"

사 진 을 찍 어 요

자, 여기 보세요!

"아, 찍지 마요. 사진 찍는 거 부끄러워."

Taking a picture

Okay, look here! "Quit it. I feel shy taking pictures."

살
금
살
금

보고 싶어 했던 영화 표와 장미꽃을 뒤에 숨기고 살금살금 다가가요.

Tiptoeing

I carefully tip-toe to you with tickets to the movie you wanted to see
and roses behind my back.

밤 하 늘

밤하늘이 참 설레어서 밖에 나왔어요.

Night sky

The night sky was magical so we came out.

folio.com/puuungi

날 씨 가 참 좋 아 서

벗나무 밑에 돗자리를 깔고 누웠어요.
당신, 너무나도 예뻐요.

Because the weather's so nice

Underneath the cherry tree, we spread out a blanket and lie on it.

You are absolutely gorgeous.

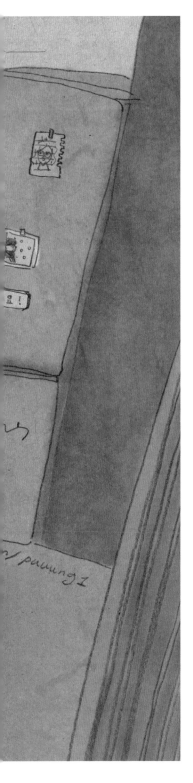

하 트 하 트 춤

"사랑해요! 하트 뿅!"
하트 모양을 만들고 빙글빙글 춤춰요!

Heart heart dance

"I love you! Heart!" I make a heart and whirl and dance!

저녁 데이트

저녁에 밖에서 데이트를 했어요.

Date night

We went out on a date at night.

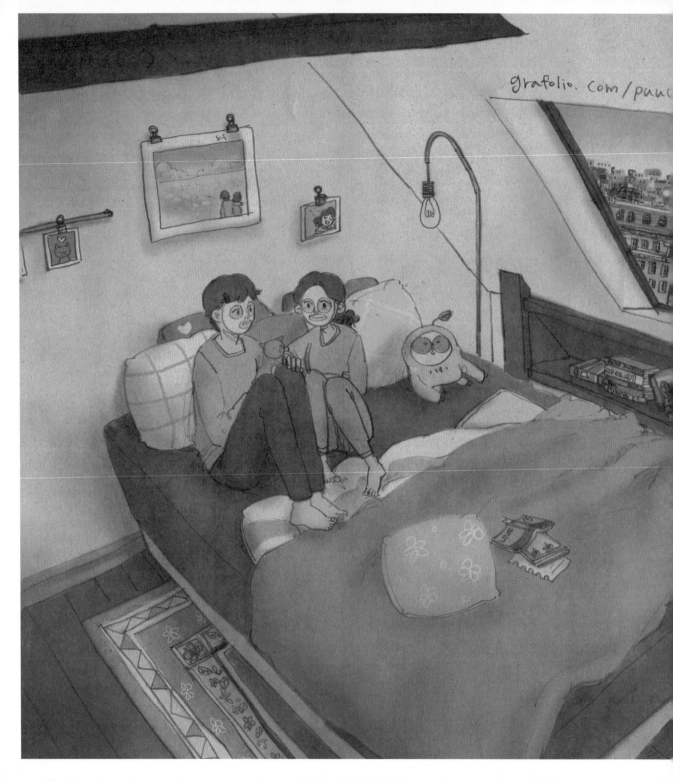

마 스 크 팩 을 해 요

같이 팩을 해요.

"이거 언제 떼요? 느낌이 이상해."

"더 붙이고 있어야 해! 내가 맨날 관리해줄게요!"

Doing face masks

We do face masks together. "When can I take this off? It feels weird."

"You have to keep it on longer! I'll pamper your face every night!"

잠

이렇게 네 심장 소리를 들으면서 자면 좋은 꿈을 꿀 것 같아.

.

Sleep

I think I'll have a sweet dream when I fall asleep listening to your heart beat like this.

쿠 키 랑
빵 만 들 기

나는 쿠키를 굽고, 너는 빵 반죽을 하고!
요리도 같이 척척 잘해요!

Making cookies and bread

I'll bake the cookies, you prepare the bread dough! We cook well together!

별 빛

예쁜 별빛 아래에서 조잘조잘 이야기를 해요.

Starry night

We chat under the pretty starlight.

너
의
책

네가 보는 책을 같이 봤어요.

"무슨 소리인지 하나도 모르겠어! 이 기호들은 대체 뭐야?"

Your book

I read the book you were reading.

"I don't know what this is about! What are these symbols?"

grafolio.com/puuung1

puuunG

아 , 혀 씹 었 어

"윽! 혀 씹었어!"

"너무 급하게 먹지 마요. 부족하면 또 만들어 줄게. 천천히 먹어요!"

Ow, I bit my tongue

"Ouch! I bit my tongue!"

"Don't eat so fast. I'll make more if we eat all this. Take your time!"

달 달 한   간 식

달달한 간식을 잔뜩 먹어요.

기분이 안 좋을 때에도

너랑 같이 달달한 간식을 먹으면 행복해져요!

Sweet desserts

We eat a bunch of sweet desserts.

Even when I'm in bad mood

I get happy after eating sweet desserts with you.

잠 시 만

잠깐 요 앞에 나갔다 올게요.

책 읽고 있어요.

쪽.

For a little while

I'll be right back. Continue reading. Smooch.

나른한 오후

나른해요.

잠깐만 눈 감고 있을게.

A sleepy afternoon

I'm sleepy. I'm going to shut my eyes for a second.

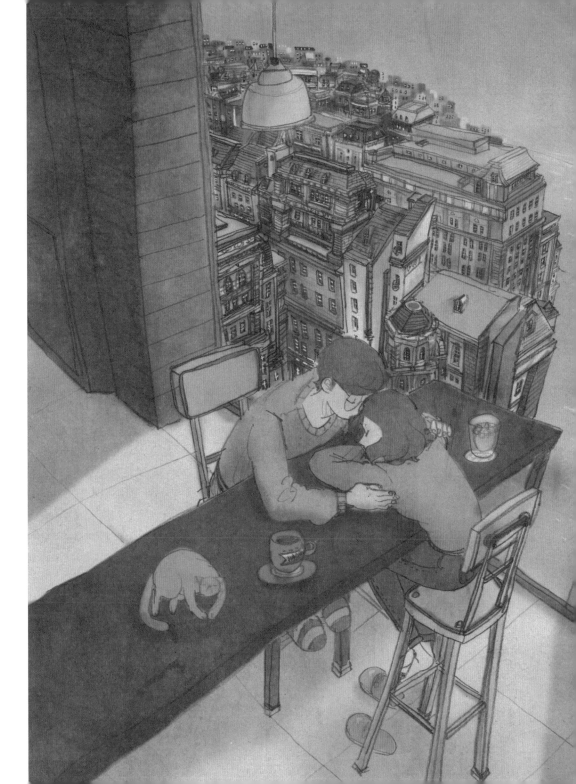

저 녁 이 오 기 전

조용히 엎드렸어요.

"방 안에서 나는 작은 소리에 귀 기울여 봐요."

Before dusk

We quietly put our heads down.

"Listen to the small sounds our room makes."

안 녕 , 안 녕 !

창밖에서 손을 흔드는 네가 보여요.
하던 일을 멈추고 너를 뚫어져라 봐요.

Hello, hello!

I see you waving from outside the window. I stop what I'm doing and fixate my eyes on you.

골
목
에
서

골목길을 걸어가다가 네가 가까이 다가왔어요.

두근두근해요!

In the alleyway

You stopped and bent close to me as we walked through an alley. My heart is pounding!

비
에
젖
었
어
요

"뛰어오느라 고생 많았어요.

이거 마시고 따뜻하게 몸 좀 녹여요."

Soaked with rain

"You must've had a hard time running through the rain.

Drink some of this and warm yourself up."

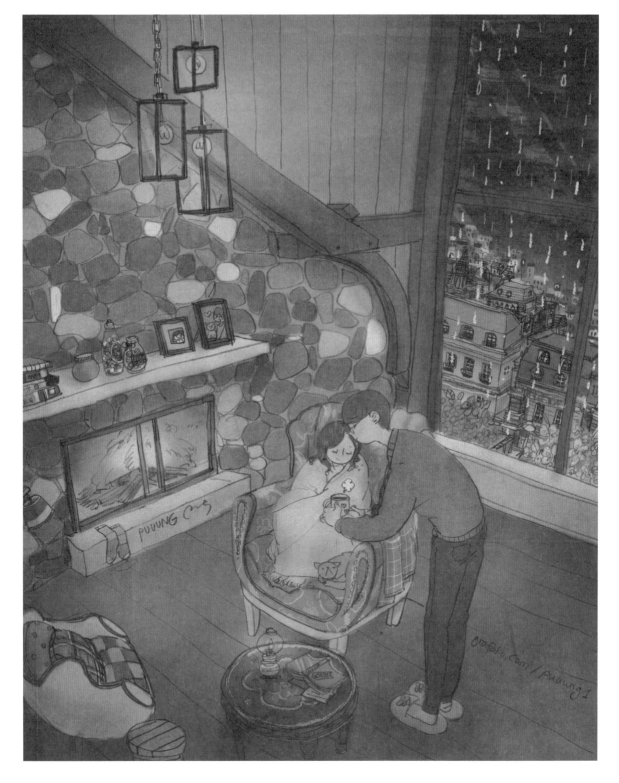

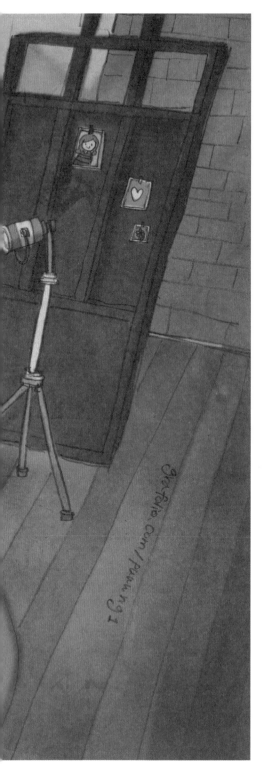

음 악 을
들 어 요

휴대폰에 스피커를 연결해놓고 음악을 들어요.

Listening to music

We connect our phone to the speaker and listen to music.

그 어떤 것도
위로가 되지 않는 날

A day when nothing can cheer me up

편
안
한

침
묵

테라스에 나왔어요.

서로 아무런 대화 없이 앉아 있어요.

말을 하지 않아도 어떤 기분인지,

어떤 생각을 하고 있는지 알 것 같아요.

Comfortable silence

We came out to the terrace. We just sit in silence.

Even when we are not talking, we seem to know

What the other person is feeling or thinking.

비 행 기
안 에 서

비행기 안에서 창문 밖을 바라봐요.

구름바다가 붉게 물들고 있네요.

"저기 봐요. 하늘을 나는 고래도 있어요!

 해가 지고 밤이 되면 별도 과연 보일까요?"

In the plane

We look out the window of the plane.

The sea of clouds is getting dyed in fiery colors.

"Look over there, there is a whale floating in the sky!

When the sun sets and night arrives, will we be able to see the stars too?"

자 요

이렇게 껴안고 하루 종일 자요.

Let's sleep

We spend the entire day falling asleep in each other's arms like this.

맛 있 어 요

"정말요? 안 이상해요?"

"맛있어! 요리 잘하는데요?"

So yummy

"Really? Are you sure it doesn't taste weird?"

"It's good! You're a pretty good cook!"

이 른 아 침

아침 일찍 일어났어요.

하늘을 봐요. 참 부드러운 색이네요.

예쁜 아침을 함께 맞이해서 좋아요.

Early morning

We woke up very early. Look at the sky, it is full of soft colors.

I'm glad to greet this pretty morning with you.

그 리 고

또 다 른 이 야 기 들

And Other stories

최근에는 그라폴리오에서 재미있는 프로젝트를 진행하고 있어요.

댓글에 달린 사연 중 매주 한 명의 이야기를 골라 그림으로 그려요.

저의 이야기를 그리는 것도 재미있지만

다른 사람의 이야기를 담는 것도 의미 있는 경험이 될 것 같아 설렙니다.

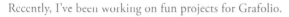

Recently, I've been working on fun projects for Grafolio.

Every week I pick an entry from all the comments sent in and draw a picture for it.

It's fun drawing my own stories,

But I'm also excited to have meaningful experiences illustrating other people's stories.

그리고 올해, 기쁘게도 첫 개인전을 열었어요.

상품 제작도 조금씩 시도하고 있고요.

I am thrilled to announce that I had my first exhibition this year.

I am even trying to create my own product line.

2016. 6.1 - 6.27

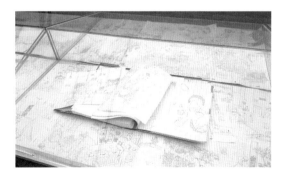

두근 두근!

예전보다 바빠지긴 했지만 저의 일상은 크게 달라지지 않았어요. 그림을 그리고, 친구나 가족들과 안부를 묻는 통화를 하고, 작업에 지치면 테라스로 나가 오밀조밀한 동네의 풍경을 바라보기도 해요. 짬을 내 좋아하는 사람들과 가까운 곳으로 나들이를 가기도 하고요.

My days have gotten busier than the past, but nothing much has really changed. I draw, keep in touch with my friends and family on the phone, And when tired I relax on the terrace while looking at the comforting view of my town. I also make time to go out and spend the day with the people I love.

길고양이였던 가필드는 이제 볼 수 없게 됐어요.

제가 먼 곳으로 이사를 와버렸거든요.

그래도 이별 뒤에는 새로운 만남이 기다리고 있어요.

새로 이사 온 곳에서 다른 길고양이들을 만났어요.

저희 학교 학생들에게 귀여움을 받고 있는 친구들이에요.

I am no longer able to see the stray cat, Garfield.

I've actually moved quite far away.

However, a new beginning awaited me.

I met other stray cats after moving to my new place.

These are the cuties adored by the students at my school.

삶을 살아간다는 게 제 그림 속 두 캐릭터처럼 늘 행복할 수는 없어요. 아주 힘들 때도, 울고 싶을 때도 많죠. 하지만 이런 생활 속에서도 저는 분명 기쁨과 행복을 느껴요. 그 소소한 순간을 감사히 여기며, 꾸준히 그림을 그리겠습니다. 여러분이 제 그림을 보는 순간만큼은 그림 속 두 주인공처럼 행복했으면 좋겠어요. 즐겁게 읽어주세요! 조만간 3권으로 다시 인사드리겠습니다. 감사합니다!

Life is not always picture-perfect like my drawings of the two characters. Times get tough, and you'll want to cry. But even in times like these, I find joy and happiness. I will continue to be thankful for the little things in life and continue drawing. At least when my readers look at my illustrations, I hope they can feel the same happiness of the two main characters. Please enjoy! I will be back soon with the third in the series. Thank you!